T5-CVF-787

Tonka®
On the Highway
STICKER BOOK

by Sonali Fry
Illustrated by Thomas LaPadula

SCHOLASTIC   Cartwheel BOOKS®

New York   Toronto   London   Auckland   Sydney
Mexico City   New Delhi   Hong Kong

No part of this publication may be reproduced, or stored in a retrieval system, or transmitted in any form or by any means, electronic, mechanical, photocopying, recording, or otherwise, without written permission of the publisher. For information regarding permission, write to Scholastic Inc., Attention: Permissions Department, 555 Broadway, New York, NY 10012.

ISBN 0-439-25912-6

TONKA® is a trademark of Hasbro, Inc.
Used with permission.
Copyright © 2001 Hasbro, Inc.
All rights reserved. Published by Scholastic Inc.
SCHOLASTIC, CARTWHEEL BOOKS and associated logos
are trademarks and/or registered trademarks of Scholastic Inc.

10 9 8 7 6 5 4 3   02 03 04 05

Printed in USA   08
First printing, May 2001

We're going on a vacation! We're taking an airplane, so we need to get to the airport. How are we going to get there?
On the highway!

Add three highway sign stickers to this scene.

Wow! There are a lot of vehicles down there. But it looks as if a few more can fit. Can you find the car sticker that will fit perfectly on this page?

Add a highway light pole on this page to the side of the road.

4

Find the fruit and vegetable truck sticker and put it in place on this page. What's in the distance? *Find the city skyline and put it in place.*

Time to pay the toll! There is a tanker trailer going through Booth 4. Can you put another one going through Booth 5?

Oops! One of the tollbooths is missing its number, and two cars are missing license plates! Can you find the right stickers and put them in place?

Now we can go over the bridge. What a sight! *Add some more trucks to the bridge.*

Do you see the ferry? There is a Tonka trash hauler on it. What other trucks do you see in this scene? Which one is the biggest?

This looks like a gas station, but there's no sign! *Can you find the correct sticker and put it on the roof? Is there a car sticker and another person you can put at the gas pump? Add a pick-up truck behind one of the cars at the pump.* Now let's eat at the Tonka Diner. But wait—its sign is missing! *Can you find it among your stickers?*

There are four tractor trailers here.
Which two are exactly the same?

These men and women are building a road. *Find a sticker of another person to help them.* The construction might slow us down a little, but once we pass it, we'll be able to go at our normal speed.

Find the right sign to put in this scene. What shape is the sticker? Add another safety barrier to the highway.

Look at that farm! Use your finger to follow the path through the field. *Add a sticker that will scare away crows. Find two bales of hay to stick in the truck. Add two pitchforks to the scene.*

17

ICES

18

Wow! A carnival! The vending trailer is selling colorful balloons, yummy ice-cream cones, and tasty hot dogs.

Find these stickers and put them on the trailer. Put the monster truck sticker on the orange gooseneck trailer.

…cars go 'round… …of them on the tr… you think will win? Can yo… and stick it in the scene?

10W-40 MOTOR OIL

RALLY

RAMP 15 SPEED

COPPER

21

Look—there's the airport! The fuel truck is filling up the airplane's tanks before it takes off.
Another airplane has just taken off.

Can you find the airplane sticker and place it in the sky?

The tug is pulling a baggage cart that is filled with pets. Can you add a cart with luggage to the train of baggage carts?

Place a ground traffic controller nearby.

Now we're getting off the highway to reach the airport. *Put the correct signs on the ramp.* This license plate is blank! Can you write your name on it?
Our trip on the highway is over. Did you have fun?